SECRETS
OF A
CHRISTMAS
ELF

BEN MILLER

SECRETS
OF A
CHRISTMAS
ELF

SIMON & SCHUSTER

First published in Great Britain in 2022 by Simon & Schuster UK Ltd

Text copyright © Passion Projects Limited 2022
Cover illustration copyright © 2022 Daniela Jaglenka Terrazzini
Interior illustrations by Christopher Naylor 2022

1 3 5 7 9 10 8 6 4 2

Simon & Schuster UK Ltd
1st Floor, 222 Gray's Inn Road, London
WC1X 8HB

www.simonandschuster.co.uk
www.simonandschuster.com.au
www.simonandschuster.co.in

Simon & Schuster Australia, Sydney
Simon & Schuster India, New Delhi
A CIP catalogue record for this book is available from the British Library.

HB ISBN 978-1-3985-1581-9
ANZ PB ISBN 978-1-3985-2362-3
eBook ISBN 978-1-3985-1582-6
eAudio ISBN 978-1-3985-1583-3

Typeset in the UK

Printed and bound by CPI Group (UK) Ltd, Croydon, CR0 4YY

To Billy, Beth, Jude and Dylan

Property of Holly Christmas, aged 155¾

This diary is <u>secret!</u>

ARE YOU EVEN LISTENING TO ME?

Sunday 28 October

Dear Diary,

Really worried about Dad.

He's not as young as he used to be. He's coming up to his 566th birthday, and I think it's all getting too much for him.

I know it's only October, but when I think of all the things he has to do before Christmas, my mind boggles.

First on the list is the grotto here at the North Pole, when he meets all the elf children of the village, marking the start of the season. Then he's off on tour around the world, visiting nurseries, schools, shopping centres, fairs and just about everything in between. If that wasn't enough, on Christmas Eve he has to deliver at least one present to every child in the entire world!

Every child on the Nice List, that is.

This morning at breakfast, he couldn't stop sneezing. I think he's coming down with something and Mum had to find him a fresh hanky. Then another one. It was gross. Not that any of my nine older brothers and sisters noticed – they were all too busy arguing over the last toffee apple.

I wish there was some way I could help him.

This morning at breakfast, he couldn't stop sneezing

Monday 29 October

I've had one of my ideas!

When I got to the Workshop, I suggested to Steinar, the Right-Hand Elf, that when December comes, I could stand in for Dad in the grotto, to give him a break. But he just laughed at me.

'Ridiculous!' he snorted. 'Imagine, all those excited elf children turning up to meet Father

Christmas, and all they get is his daughter Holly! There'll be riots!'

'But listen!' I said excitedly, as an idea began to take shape. 'I could disguise myself as him! I could put on a false beard and stuff a cushion up my jacket.'

Steinar pulled a face. Now that Ola, the Left-Hand Elf, was in prison for stealing toys, Steinar was in charge of practically everything to do with Christmas. And, in my opinion, it had gone to his head.

'Children aren't stupid, you know,' he sniffed. 'You've got no wrinkles. They'd guess straight away.'

'Why don't you do it, then?' I replied. 'You've got loads.'

Steinar's eyes widened, and I realised I must have said something rude.

'Sorry,' I added hastily. 'That came out wrong.'

'May I remind you,' he said tetchily, 'that whoever your parents may be, you remain a *junior* toymaking elf. And a fairly mediocre one at that, judging by your recent toy quotas. Drones are going to be really popular this year, and yesterday you only made 6,492 of them. You worry about your work, and leave me to worry about Father Christmas.'

Tuesday 30 October

One day till Halloween!

There's going to be a party on the ice rink, where everyone dresses up as their favourite scary character. It's the last chance for us Workshop Elves to blow off some steam before the Christmas rush, and we all make lots of effort with our costumes.

During our hot-chocolate-and-marshmallow break this morning, I decided to tell my best friend Tog I was going as Taffeta Hound, the Naughtiest Girl Alive. She's famous here at the North Pole, because she's been on the Naughty List every year since she was born. That means she has never, ever had a present from Father Christmas!

Naughty List

1. *Taffeta Hound*
2. *William C. Hill*
3. *Lucy Patterson*
4. *Charles Wilson*
5. *Annabel Kappa*

In fact, a couple of years ago — I remember, because it made the headline of the *North Pole News* — she put her younger brother in the washing machine on Christmas Eve! She pressed the button to turn the machine on, and if her grandmother hadn't happened to check up on her, he'd have been boil-washed with their baby sister's nappies. My dad was so cross that instead of a present, he gave Taffeta a piece of coal in her stocking. He's always threatening to do that to naughty kids and gives in at the last minute, but this time he actually followed through.

When I told Tog about my plan to go to the Halloween party dressed as Taffeta, he went quiet.

'Oh,' he said. 'I thought we might go together.'

'Really?' I asked. 'As what?'

'Max and Ola.'

I guess I need to explain who Max and Ola are.

Basically, they're baddies and last year, they tried to steal Christmas!

It was a huge scandal, because Ola was Dad's Left-Hand Elf, which is a really important job and Dad trusted him. And *I* really trusted Max. He was a Workshop Elf just like me and Tog, and he and I used to be ice-skating partners.

Anyway, it turned out that Ola was really Grimm Grimmsson in disguise! He used to be a big businessman at the North Pole, making shoes for humans, but he went bankrupt and stole his workers' pensions. Max is his son, and the two of them were secretly plotting to steal all the toys and sell them. They said it was to make money, but I think the real reason was because they were jealous of Dad. Giving away toys has made him really famous and popular, and the whole Grimmsson family have it in for him.

Luckily Tog and I found out, and we managed to stop them just at the last minute in a super scary sleigh chase. We were even famous ourselves – for a while.

'I could be Ola,' said Tog, 'and you could be Max.'

'Hmm. I'm not sure,' I said, thinking it over.

'Why not?' asked Tog. 'I've got really good at masks. I could make us look just like them.'

Tog's speciality is sewing toy lemurs, but recently he's been branching out into giant anteater masks. You wouldn't think many kids would ask for one of those for Christmas, but they've been very popular in Finland.

'What if people think we're showing off?' I asked. 'Because we caught them.'

'Ah,' Tog said, and went quiet for a bit. 'I sort of might have made my costume already.'

'Well, so have I,' I said, which was true. Taffeta Hound has ginger hair and freckles, or at least she did in the photo I saw that time in the *North Pole News*. I had borrowed a ginger wig and made it into two plaits, and found one of my sister Sniff's old dresses that had just the right kind of light blue check. I had even made a pretend washing machine out of an old cardboard box, and put one of my dolls in it to look like Taffeta Hound's younger brother!

'Please, Holly,' said Tog.

'Look,' I said. 'If you want to go with someone

14

else, I really don't mind. But I'd like to go as Taffeta Hound.'

We changed the subject, but I could tell he was a bit upset.

I hope I've made the right decision.

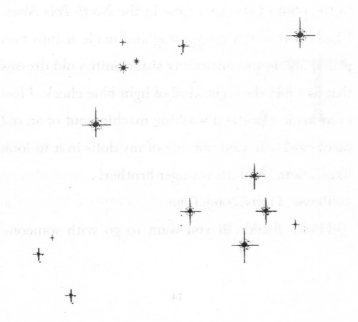

Wednesday 31 October

Tog asked me if I minded him going to the Halloween costume party with Fizz.

Fizz is one of the new Workshop Elves, and I really like her. She's even better at electronics than I am. And coding. And design. And remote controls. They brought her in to replace Max, who used to make VR headsets.

Tog explained that she'd look really good dressed in Max's costume because she's slim with green eyes, just like Max.

Some elves might feel jealous that their best friend is going to the Halloween costume party with someone else, but luckily I'm not that kind of elf.

Anyway, I'd better go because I need to get ready.

Just back from the Halloween party. It was so much fun!

A weird thing happened though.

As soon as we'd finished at the Workshop,

I rushed home to get changed into my Taffeta Hound costume. Mum even let me borrow her eyebrow pencil so I could add freckles.

Then I went crunching out into the snow to join the party.

It's quite a long way from our house to the village, and the snow was piled high on either side of the track. As I entered the forest, a dog sleigh came skittering round the bend. My heart skipped a beat. Side by side on the front seat were Max and Ola!

A chill bristled up my spine as I remembered them hijacking Dad's sleigh last Christmas Eve. Then I realised it must be Tog and Fizz in disguise!

'Woah, there!' I called out, blocking their way.

Side by side on the front seat were Max and Ola!

They pulled on the reins, and skidded to a halt.

'Hi, Tog! Hi, Fizz!' I called.

The two figures looked behind them, puzzled.

'Are you talking to us?' asked Tog. Whatever I thought about him going to the party with Fizz instead of me, I couldn't fault his commitment to the role. He had made himself a mask that looked just like Ola, and he was doing something with his voice so that he even *sounded* like him!

'You're going the wrong way!' I called. 'The ice rink's that way!'

'The ice rink?' repeated Fizz, pulling a face. Her costume was really good too, and she looked and sounded exactly like Max.

'Aren't you going to the party?' I asked. 'I love your outfits – especially the overalls. They look just like the ones they have in prison.'

The two figures looked at one another.

'Ye-es,' said Tog carefully, grinning at Fizz. 'That's exactly where we're going. To the Halloween party. Dressed as those two notorious scoundrels, Ola and Max!'

They laughed, and I joined in, because their costumes really were very good.

'See you on the ice!' bellowed Tog, and he cracked his whip at the dogs, completely in character.

'Yeah, we'll be right along,' added Fizz, still doing Max's voice.

I watched them drive away, laughing and nudging

one another, and for a tiny moment I felt a little bit left out. Part of me wondered whether I wanted to go to the party at all. But I carried on walking, and the snow looked so pretty, sparkling on the trees, that I soon felt better. By the time I reached the village, and I saw other elves in costume heading for the ice rink, I felt excited all over again about being Taffeta Hound. But the moment I arrived, guess who I bumped into?

Tog and Fizz!

Dressed as a lady and a sheep!

'Wow!' I said. 'Why did you change costumes?'

Tog looked confused

'Don't you remember?' I asked. 'I saw you just now in the lane, dressed as Ola and Max. And now you're here! Dressed as . . .' My voice trailed off, because I wasn't really sure what they'd come as.

'Bo Peep and one of her sheep,' explained Fizz quickly. 'Going as Ola and Max seemed a bit mean so I talked Tog out of it. Look, I borrowed a hula hoop from the Workshop and sewed it into the bottom of my dress.'

'And I had lots of wool left over from my lemurs,' explained Tog.

'Careful,' said Tog, as Fizz prodded him with her crook

'Plus you've got quite prominent front teeth,' added Fizz. 'Ooh, look! Let's grab a glass of that spooky green punch.'

'Careful,' said Tog, as Fizz prodded him with her crook.

'I don't want to lose my sheep, do I?' Fizz grinned.

Tog didn't answer. In fact, for a moment he looked quite cross.

All of which made me wonder who I'd bumped into on the lane . . .

Thursday 1 November

There was a bit of an atmosphere at the Workshop today.

Tog and Fizz weren't talking to one another. I'm not sure exactly why, but I think it's something to do with Halloween.

At cinnamon-toast break, Tog went off to sit on his own, and Fizz followed him, asking what was wrong. Tog muttered something about feeling silly in his sheep costume, and Fizz said, 'How exactly is that my fault?' Then they refused to speak to one another for the rest of the day, which was quite tricky because the three of us share a workbench.

'Would you ask Fizz to pass the sticky tape?' Tog asked, as he was packaging up one of his anteater masks.

'Would you ask Tog to pass it back, please?' Fizz would say, a few minutes later.

'Will you two stop it?' I huffed. 'You're slowing me down!'

Tog was about to reply, when we were all distracted by a commotion at the far end of the Workshop. Tingle, who makes board games, was reading from a fresh copy of the *North Pole News*, and a crowd of elves had gathered round him.

'Cloudberry Break Out,' announced Tingle, and all the elves gasped in surprise. 'Ola and Max Grimmsson, the former Workshop Elves who tried to steal Christmas last year, have escaped from Cloudberry Maximum Security Prison.'

More gasps. One elf clapped his hand to his forehead in shock. I felt the hairs on my arms stand on end. I must have seen the *real* Ola and Max on the way to the party!

'Their cell was discovered empty this morning, with its window bars sawn clean through. Security camera footage shows that that they were recently visited by a mysterious blonde-haired woman wearing sunglasses and a headscarf, who spoke with a Luxembourgian accent and signed herself in as "Madame Appleklatzen". This is now thought to be a made-up name, as appleklatzen is a type of cake popular in Luxembourg. Police are working on the assumption that she concealed a hacksaw in such a cake, which she brought to the prison as a gift.'

'Luxembourg,' mused Tingle. 'Didn't they vote for never-ending Christmas?'

It was true. A woman called Eva Klutsch had

NEWS
LATE EDITION November 1st

...K OUT
Tax Grimmsson
Security Prison

Today's Weather:
SNOW

been elected President, and her main policy was for every day to be Christmas Day. It sounded great to me, but Dad had been really cross.

'Christmas Day comes once a year,' he had said. 'That's what makes it special. Just because she says it's Christmas all year, it doesn't make it true. I'll still be delivering my presents on Christmas Eve, whatever she does.'

I decided I had better tell Dad the news about Max and Ola escaping, and I rushed up to his office. But Steinar said he'd gone home. His cold had gone to his chest and he needed some rest.

When I got home after work, Dad had already gone up to bed.

Now I'm really worried.

I have never, ever known him to miss a single hour of work before.

I have to help him. But how? There's no one who can do his job apart from him.

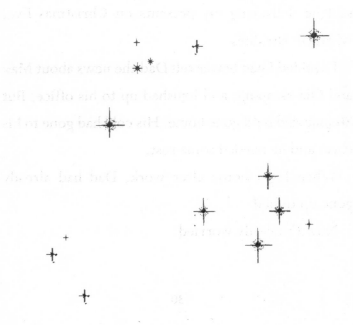

Saturday 3 November

I've had the most amazing idea for how to help Dad! I'm going to build a robot that looks just like him to help with all his Christmas duties!

Sunday 4 November

My idea is rubbish.

Monday 5 November

Feeling a bit more confident today. Plucked up the courage to tell Tog about my robot, and he was really encouraging. In fact, he wants to help! He offered to make a mask for the robot to wear. I said I wasn't sure how the elf children would react to a Father Christmas with the face of an anteater – but Tog promised me it would look just like Dad. To prove it, he showed me the masks of Max and Ola he'd made for Halloween. They were really good! We put them on for fun and made each other laugh.

Tog's one of my best friends and I'm so grateful he cares about helping Dad.

Tuesday 6 November

Tog and I spent our whole lunchtime working on the robot designs. It's going to need to do all the things that Dad does, so it's quite a complex job. It's fun spending time with Tog, too.

Wednesday 7 November

Worried that Fizz is feeling left out. After Tog and I finished work for the day, we started building the hardware for the robot. As Fizz was leaving, I caught a strange look in her eye. I know Tog went to the party with her instead of me *and* she made Tog feel silly dressed up as a sheep — but I still feel bad.

Thursday 8 November

Asked Fizz if she would like to help us with the robot, and she smiled and gave me a big hug!

Monday 12 November

There's been no time to write in my diary this weekend as Tog, Fizz and I have been working non-stop on the robot. Really glad I asked Fizz to join the team. She's made a VR headset that can control him! When you put it on, you see through the robot's eyes and hear through its ears.

She says it might come in handy if we need to override the remote control.

Just a few more days and he'll be finished. Then all we need to do is test him. It's just as well, because I can tell Dad's really stressed about Christmas. He tried to sneak out this morning to go to work, but Mum heard him coughing in the boot room and sent him back to bed. Obviously only Dad can deliver the presents, but the robot could easily give out the toys in the grotto and handle some of the tour dates. Then, with the pressure off, Dad could focus on getting well for the big day. He's very proud though, so I need to find the right moment to tell him.

Tuesday 13 November

Got told off by Steinar, the Right-Hand Elf. He said my quotas have dropped too far, and gave me an official warning! It was really embarrassing – I mean I'm Father Christmas's daughter! I think it's because my mind's taken up with making the robot. Yesterday, during Workshop hours, I only made 6,297 drones. What if Steinar tells Dad and it makes him even more worried?

Decided I need to put the robot on hold for a bit while I focus on my toymaking.

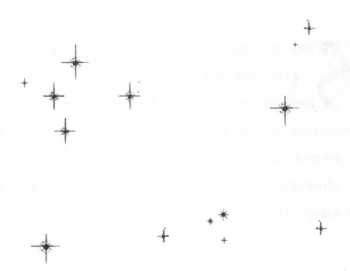

Thursday 15 November

Something really weird happened last night.

I decided to get an early night, so I'd be fresh for toymaking this morning. I was lying in my bed, staring at the moon (I like it really cold in my bedroom or I can't sleep, so I always leave the window half-open), when I heard Frosty, our dog, barking outside.

It was the sort of bark she makes when she sees an intruder. I tried calling to her, but she ignored me, so I crept downstairs. My brothers and sisters were all having strawberry waffles in the kitchen, so I snuck past the doorway and slipped outside.

Frosty came bounding towards me, barking excitedly, then turned and stared into the darkness, with her ears forward and her tail held high, as if she could hear someone. At the far end of our property, near the gate that leads to the frozen lake, I saw two shadowy figures.

One was short and thick-set, the other was tall and thin.

'Hey!' I called. 'Who's there?'

The short figure nudged the taller one, and they

slunk away into the darkness. I ran back to the kitchen and told everyone what I had seen.

'I saw them!' I yelled. 'Max and Ola!'

'Who?' asked my sister Sniff, squirting my brother Whittle in the eye with caramel sauce.

'The escaped convicts – the ones who tried to steal Christmas!'

'Yeah, yeah, Holly,' my sister Pickle said snidely. 'You and Tog saved Christmas last year, we all remember.'

'You don't understand,' I urged. 'They're outside, watching the house! I think they might be up to something. Didn't you hear Frosty barking?'

'Are you sure you didn't dream it?' asked my brother Pocket, forming his words like I was a baby and couldn't understand Elvish.

'Holly! What are you doing up?' asked Mum. She was carrying a tea tray with untouched food on it, and I guessed she had been upstairs, looking after Dad. 'I thought you were having an early night?'

'I heard something!' I protested.

'And you'll hear something else in a minute, if you don't get up those stairs.' She lowered her voice. 'Don't forget you got an official warning from Steinar. Your Father will be mortified if he finds out. He has enough to worry about!'

Suddenly all nine of my brothers and sisters were paying rapt attention. 'Wooooooo!' they all said. 'Holly's in trouble!'

I ran back up the stairs, ears burning with the injustice of it all.

The wind was whistling loudy through my open window, so I slammed the sash down, pulled my curtains tight and buried my face in my pillow.

Being the youngest is really rubbish sometimes.

Friday 16 November

A big surprise this morning at breakfast.

'Holly, look!' said Mum, holding up her copy of the *North Pole News*. I read the headline out loud.

'EX-XMAS-ELVES CAPTURED AND RETURNED TO PRISON!'

'You were right!' Mum exclaimed. 'It *was* Max

and Ola you saw. They've been arrested. See?'

My lips twitched as I skimmed the article. Apparently, Max and Ola had been found fast asleep in a cave in the Arctic Hills and were now safely back in prison. There was a photo of them, dressed in their prison overalls.

I couldn't help but feel relieved. I just *knew* they were up to no good.

Saturday 17 November

Dad joined us for breakfast today. It was so good to see him up and about, although he looks very tired and thin. He's been getting daily updates from Steinar, and he's worried the schedule is falling behind.

When he was going through his post, he found a letter from his agent. That's the person who books all of his personal appearances before Christmas. She's called Samira and it's very hard to read her handwriting, so everyone at the breakfast table – that's me, my nine brothers and sisters, Mum and Dad – had a turn at trying to work out what it said.

'I can't make head nor tail of it,' said Dad, passing it on.

'Her pet hamster is having babies,' announced my oldest brother, Whittle, decisively.

Pickle, one of my middle sisters, glanced at the card. 'She's learning to whistle.'

Sprocket put her reading glasses on. She was only one hundred and sixty, but she had worn glasses since she was eighty-seven. 'She's stranded on a desert island made of cheese.'

'She's raising money for a racoon sanctuary,' said Thistle flatly.

Finally, it was my turn. I'd always been good at reading Samira's postcards. I went to a special place in my head, and suddenly the words un-knotted themselves, revealing the message! I hesitated. It was bad news. 'She's added more dates to your tour,' I said, looking at Dad. 'In Iceland.'

'Let me see that,' asked Mum, worried, taking the card.

'Hmmm,' said Dad thoughtfully.

'Holly's right,' said Mum. 'That's exactly what it says.'

Dad was quiet for a bit. 'Hmmm,' he said again. Then he had a coughing fit. Then he was quiet for a bit again. I sneaked a glance at his plate. He hadn't even touched his French toast, and normally he has at least six slices.

'Hmmm . . .' he mused, for a third time.

'Say it,' prodded Mum, knowing there was something on his mind.

'I think I should go.'

'Torvil, you can't add more dates. You're still getting over this sick bug; you need to take it easy!'

'Don't you worry, my darling,' said Dad, squeezing Mum's hand. 'And don't you worry either, Holly. The magic of Christmas will get me through.'

I felt words rising up inside me, like bubbles in soda. *I've made a robot! That can stand in for you at the grotto!* But I managed to hold them down.

It's not ready yet, and anyway, Mum's right —
I need to focus on my toymaking.

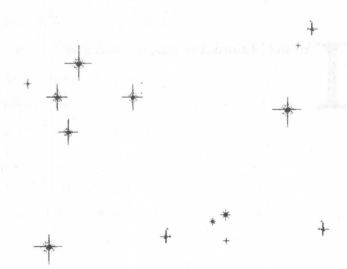

Sunday 18 November

I'm sick! I think I've caught Dad's cold.

Tuesday 20 November

Been in bed for days. Snotted my way through a whole box of tissues and my nostrils sting when I sneeze. Which is pretty much all the time.

Wednesday 21 November

S till ill. One-and-a-half boxes of tissues. I'm going to be really behind at the Workshop!

Thursday 22 November

Two boxes. A personal best.

Friday 23 November

At 2:34 p.m. this afternoon, my left nostril finally stopped running, closely followed by my right nostril at 2:55 p.m. Then at 3:05 p.m. my left nostril started again and I got through three more boxes of tissues.

Tuesday 27 November

Still coughing. Three quarters of a box.

Wednesday 28 November

Finally, I feel a little bit better.

I came downstairs so I could read my book by the fire and saw that the Christmas decorations are up! Garlands of holly with sparkling red berries were draped either side of the fireplace, set with twinkling candles. I was so happy to see them there, but it also made me a bit sad, because I had missed out on dressing the tree – one of my favourite things in the whole world. I usually get to do it with my brothers and sisters, singing songs and arguing over what should go where. But because I was ill in bed they must have done it without me.

I was just settling down, when who should walk in but Dad!

'I wonder if you might help me?' He beamed, holding up a toy fairy. She was wearing a bright white ballgown and holding a silver wand that matched her silver wings. 'I'm wondering where we might put this young lady.'

'You saved her!' I gasped. 'For me!'

Chuckling, Dad lifted me up under my arms, and

I fastened the fairy to the top of the tree. She looked magnificent.

Dad explained that he had come home specially to look after me, and we spent all day together. At lunchtime, he made us both hazelnut spread and banana toasties, and in the afternoon he read my book to me. It's called *The Night Before Christmas*, and it's a sort of poemy-story about a human who sees Dad delivering presents. My copy has been passed down through all my brothers and sisters and the cover is torn, but that makes me love it all the more. Dad read it in his special Grown-up Reading Voice, and when he got to the bit of the story where he arrives, he got so carried away that he started coughing again.

'Goodness me!' he exclaimed, once he had recovered his breath. 'Don't tell your mother, but I just can't seem to shake this thing.'

That reminded me about my robot. Before I knew what I was doing, I told Dad all about my plan, and how worried I've been, in case Christmas is getting too much for him now that he's really old.

He laughed when I said that, and his eyes twinkled in a way they haven't done for ages.

'I'm not as ancient as all that,' he chortled. 'My father, bless his soul, lived to be one thousand three hundred and sixty-five, so there's a little more Christmas magic in me yet. But I have been a bit run down lately, and this might be just the sort of solution I'm looking for.'

'Really?' I asked.

'Of course!' he replied. 'It's a very clever and thoughtful idea.'

He smiled and looked me straight in the eye. It felt like he was reading my thoughts.

'I hope you know, Holly,' he said, 'how talented you are. And that you'd be a Christmas Elf whoever your parents were.'

I felt a lump in my throat, so I just nodded.

He tapped my chest, just by my heart. 'There's magic in here,' he said gently. 'You just need to believe in it.'

My eyes started to burn, and I pushed my face into the shoulder of his velvet jacket. All my stress and worry melted away, and I started to sob.

'Believe in yourself, Holly Christmas,' said Dad, hugging me tight.

Thursday 29 November

Mum says I can go back to work tomorrow! Tog and Fizz called round to see how I was, and I told them that Dad wants to try the robot out. The only problem is time. There's just two days to go before the grotto opens!

Tog suggested we record Dad's voice, so that the

robot can speak, and the three of us went to his study to ask his permission.

'Well, well, if it isn't Tog and Fizz.' He beamed. 'I hear you've been helping my daughter with this robot of hers.'

Tog and Fizz suddenly went very shy, so I spoke for them.

'That's right,' I said. 'And we'd like to record your voice so the robot can speak to the elf children that visit you in the grotto.'

'I see,' said Dad, pulling a serious face. The colour had come back to his cheeks and he was his old mischevious self again. 'In that case, you need to record seven sentences.'

'Only seven?' I asked.

'I don't know if you've ever heard me in the grotto meeting the elf children,' he continued. 'But it's a little bit . . .' he searched for the right word. 'Repetitive,' he concluded. 'Tog, start the voice recorder, and I'll give you everything you need.'

Tog fiddled with the controls and held the microphone close.

'Are we rolling?' asked Dad.

Tog nodded.

'Ho ho ho!' said Dad. 'Hello there, and what might your name be? Have you been good? What would you like for Christmas? I'll see what I can do. Now let me give you a little something to be going on with. Goodbye, and don't forget to leave me a mince pie and a drink, and a carrot for the reindeer!'

Dad gave a thumbs up, and Tog stopped recording.

'That should do it,' he said, nodding. 'I don't know why no one thought of this before!'

Just at that moment, there was a knock at the door, and Steinar entered.

'Oh, hello,' he said, sounding slightly disappointed to see me, Tog and Fizz in Dad's study.

'These three young elves have had the most marvellous idea,' said Dad. 'They've made a robot to take over from me in the grotto.'

There was a pause while confusion, then irritation, flitted across Steinar's face. Closely followed by a large fake smile.

'What an excellent idea!' he agreed.

Friday 30 November

Disaster!

I've really messed up!

I'd better start at the beginning . . .

After work, Tog, Fizz and I put the finishing touches to the robot. It really does look a lot like Dad, except its face doesn't move very much and its hat keeps falling off. Then we set it up in the grotto so we could try it out.

We sat it on Dad's special chair, next to the sack of presents. Tog pretended to be one of the Grotto elves, and Fizz and I pretended to be elf children.

I went first.

'Another visitor for you, Father Christmas!' announced Tog, leading me towards the robot.

'Ho ho ho!' said the robot, swivelling its face away from me.

'Hi, Father Christmas,' I said.

'Hello there, and what might your name be?' said the robot, raising and lowering one arm for no particular reason.

I carried on talking, even though it was looking away from me.

'Holly,' I said.

The robot stood up and sat down again.

'Have you been good?' it asked.

'Yes,' I said.

The robot's head swivelled to look at me. The coloured bits of its eyes made a full circle, and I have to admit, the effect was slightly frightening.

'What would you like for Christmas?' it asked. Its eyelids opened and closed several times, and its rubber mouth smiled. The mask creased a bit and I glimpsed the metal gums around its gleaming white teeth.

'Err . . . a basketball hoop,' I replied. Which was something I actually was thinking of putting on my Christmas list.

'I'll see what I can do,' said the robot, and its head went all the way round, ending up more or less back where it started. 'Now let me give you a little something to be going on with.'

Before I knew what was happening, the robot picked me up, and stuffed me face down into the sack of presents!

'Goodbye!' I heard its muffled voice say. 'And don't forget to leave me a mince pie and a drink, and a carrot for the reindeer.'

It then started running all its words together, and stuffed Fizz in the sack beside me!

We spent the rest of the evening trying to fix it.

There's no way out now . . . the grotto opens tomorrow!

Saturday 1 December

I'm so upset, I can hardly write. But I need to tell someone what's happened. So here goes . . . The first day in the grotto actually went really well. The repairs we made last night seem to have worked, and although the robot is still a bit jerky, and doesn't always look at the person it's talking to, and once got up and did press-ups in the middle of a visit for no apparent reason, it all went okay.

There was a really long queue of elf children and, amazingly, none of them seemed to realise they were meeting a robot and not Father Christmas! And if they don't notice, the children on the world tour certainly won't! The robot even managed to give them each a little present, rather than stuffing them all in the sack.

But then things took a terrible turn.

Dad had been watching the grotto from his office – he has screens up there where he can see everything that's going on at Christmas Place – and after the last elf child went home, we went up to see what he thought of it all.

But his office was empty.

Instead, on the desk, was a cut-up copy of the article from the *North Pole News* about Max and Ola, the one with the headline 'EX-XMAS-ELVES CAPTURED AND RETURNED TO PRISON!'

Lots of letters had been cut out and made into a message by sticking them on a piece of paper. The message had been fastened to the back of Dad's chair, so it was clear that it was about him.

It read:

hAND OvER All TOyS oN XMAS EVE OR ELSE

Below the message, someone had glued the photo from the paper of Max and Ola, and a picture of an old-fashioned castle, perched high on a hill.

We were trying to figure out exactly what it all meant, when Steinar arrived.

'I've got three elf children crying downstairs because your robot grabbed their presents and stuffed them back into the sack!' he said huffily. Then he saw the look on our faces.

'What's happened?' he asked.

'Someone's taken Dad,' I said, pointing at the empty chair.

Steinar snatched the message. His eyes darted from side to side, and all the colour drained from his face. Then his voice changed and he said quietly, 'Tog. Fizz. Go home.'

'Why?' I asked.

'Because your father's been kidnapped,' said Steinar gravely. 'By Max and Ola. Just like last time, they want the toys. Unless we hand them over on Christmas Eve, then . . .' His voice trailed away.

'Then what?' I asked.

'I shudder to think.'

The rest is a bit of a blur. I remember Tog and Fizz slinking to the door, and Steinar calling Mum to tell her what had happened. I couldn't hear what she said, but I could tell from the tone of her voice that she was very upset.

'Come on,' said Steinar. 'I'll take you home.'

Mum was waiting for me at the front door and

gave me a big hug. Steinar must have told my brothers and sisters too, because they soon started to arrive, one by one, all of them looking shocked and sad. After lots more hugs, we gathered in the dining room, the place where Dad always holds his big Christmas Lunches.

All the decorations were up in there too, with wreaths of holly – my favourite, because Mum and Dad named me after it – and giant bunches of mistletoe swinging from the rafters. Usually it's one of my favourite places in the entire world, but with Dad in such grave danger, I just felt numb.

Steinar stood on a chair and addressed us all.

'As you all know, Father Christmas has disappeared, and this –' he held up the piece of paper we had found in Dad's office — 'appears to be some sort of ransom note. I've just got off the phone with the governor of Cloudberry Prison. Sadly, he has confirmed that the two men they captured are decoys.'

'Decoys?' repeated Mum.

'They aren't the real Max and Ola,' explained Steinar. 'They're just two lookalikes. From Luxembourg.'

'What?' asked Whittle.

'How is that possible?' added Sniff.

'I don't know,' admitted Steinar. 'But I intend to find out. In the meantime, we have to treat this kidnapping as real, with Ola and Max as the culprits. The question is, how are we going to respond?'

'What do you mean?' I asked.

'The message is clear,' explained Steinar. 'Max and Ola are holding your father in this castle in Luxembourg. So you have a choice. Give them the toys and get your father back, or don't give them the toys . . .' Steinar broke off, not wanting to complete the thought that was forming in his mind. 'And face the consequences.'

Mum gasped in horror.

'That's not a choice!' I protested. 'That's horrible!'

'What can I say?' Steinar said. 'These are desperate individuals with a terrible grudge.'

'I don't understand,' I said. 'Last year Max and Ola tried to steal Christmas. This year they've kidnapped Dad! Why? What is it they want?'

'Revenge,' said Mum, 'Pure and simple. Ola may have changed his name, but he hasn't changed his nature. As Grimm Grimmsson, he used to run the North Pole for profit. Now your father's in charge, giving everything away for free. Ola hates your father, and so does Max.'

'I'm sorry to ask, Mother Christmas,' pressed Steinar. 'But what's your decision? Hand over the toys?'

Mum was silent for a few moments, then shook her head. 'Torvil would never agree to that.'

'But if we don't . . .'

We all exchanged worried looks.

'There's got to be another way,' I said. 'What if we break in there somehow, and help Dad escape?'

84

'Never going to happen,' said Steinar, shaking his head. 'You know who this castle belongs to, don't you?'

We didn't.

'It's the family home of Eva Klutsch, the newly elected President of Luxembourg.'

'Wait!' I said, interrupting him. 'The one who promised Christmas every day?'

'The very same,' replied Steinar. 'Holstein Castle has been her family's home for more than six hundred years, and throughout all that time, no one has ever broken in. It's defended by a private army called the Holstein Guard.'

'Wait a minute,' I said, my mind reeling. 'Did you say Luxembourg?'

Steinar nodded.

'What does this woman look like?' I asked.

Steinar tapped at his mobile phone, then held up a photo.

'That's her!' I exclaimed. 'Look, everyone, just like the photo in the *North Pole News*. She must be the woman who helped Max and Ola escape from prison!'

Mum sighed and sank into a chair. Sensing something was wrong, Frosty jumped up, putting her paws on Mum's lap.

'Don't worry, Mum,' I said. 'We've got this. Okay, so what do we know about Holstein Castle? We must have delivered presents there.'

'Never,' replied Steinar, shaking his head. 'Each

and every ancestor of Eva Klutsch has been on the Naughty List, even when they were babies.'

Everyone looked at one another, as if we had reached a dead end.

'What about the two lookalikes?' I asked. 'Maybe they can help us . . . ? How did they end up in prison instead of Max and Ola?'

My eldest brother, Whittle, held up his hand, telling me to stop. 'Don't worry, Steinar,' he said confidently. 'Christmas is not going to be cancelled. Far from it, it's going to be even bigger and better than last year. We're going to go to Holstein Castle and get Dad back, without paying a single toy.'

'Who's "we"?' I asked, feeling like I already knew the answer.

'Your brothers and sisters and me.'

'And what about me?' I floundered. 'Can't I come?'

Whittle shook his head. 'You're too young.'

'No, I'm not!' I protested.

'It's too risky,' said Whittle.

'Please!' I begged.

But Whittle wouldn't listen. 'And no blabbing,' he said. 'If this is going to work, it has to be secret.'

'There's one small problem,' said Steinar importantly, and we all turned to look at him. 'The tour starts in three days' time. Torvil has to be back by then, or thousands of children are going to be disappointed.'

'No problem,' said Whittle firmly. 'We'll be back with Dad in twenty-four hours.'

Sunday 2 December

I t was chaos today.

Word must have somehow gotten out about what had happened, because there were no Guard Elves at the gates like there usually are, and when I entered the courtyard, I saw that every elf in Christmas Place was crowded around the steps of Christmas House.

Steinar was standing on the top step, speaking to the crowd through a megaphone.

'Many of you will already have heard—' he began, before there was a loud screech of feedback. A nearby elf stepped in, fiddled with the controls, then handed the megaphone back.

'Ahem,' Steinar said, clearing his throat. 'And I really don't want anyone panicking about this . . .'

An expectant hush fell over the crowd.

'But Father Christmas has been kidnapped.'

No sooner had his words left the loudspeaker, than elves began screaming, running left and right! Some surged up the steps, knocking Steinar flat, banging on the locked doors. Others ran in circles around the courtyard, bumping into one another. More still began climbing the drainpipes of Christmas House for safety.

Somehow I found Tog and Fizz in the crowd.

'What happened?' asked Tog. 'After we left you?'

I nearly blurted it all out, how my brothers and sisters had left for Luxembourg to try to get Dad back. But then I remembered my promise. All of it had to stay a secret!

'It's true,' I said. 'Ola and Max have kidnapped Dad.'

'But how?' asked Fizz. 'They're both locked up in prison.'

'No. They're not,' I countered. 'That was a trick they played. So that we would all stop looking for them.'

'I don't understand,' said Tog.

'It wasn't Max and Ola they found hiding in that cave in the Arctic Hills,' I explained. 'It was two lookalikes. From Luxembourg.'

'Those two!' exclaimed Tog. 'They're so sneaky.'

'Mind blown,' whistled Fizz. She was tapping her foot on the floor nervously.

A large Tech Elf suddenly knocked Tog sideways. 'Don't panic!' he yelled. 'Don't panic!' Then went rushing off again.

'Look,' I said, helping Tog to his feet. 'The Workshop's closed today. Why don't we go to Cloudberry and investigate?'

Luckily enough, when we arrived at the prison it was still visiting time, and after passing our security checks, we were shown into a large room where lots of Prisoner Elves were meeting with their families.

Sitting at one of the tables, their heads almost touching the ceiling, their bottoms squished into chairs that were much too small for them, were two humans that looked exactly like Max and Ola!

They were such good lookalikes – even though they were much bigger than regular elves – that we were too scared to go and introduce ourselves at first. But then I remembered that as well as my dad's freedom, the whole of Christmas was at stake, and I bravely took the plunge.

'Holly Christmas,' I announced in my most confident voice. 'These are my friends, Tog Harket and Fizz Bump.'

'Arno Bruch,' said the one that looked like Ola,

standing politely, the back of his head pressed against the ceiling. 'And this is Wouter Trontheim.'

'We want to ask you some questions,' I began.

'Not at all,' said Wouter, the one that looked like Max. 'We'd be delighted to answer. Then we have a question of our own, if you'd be so kind.'

'First things first,' I said. 'How come you two are in here, and not Max and Ola?'

Arno and Wouter looked at one another, to see which of them wanted to answer first.

'We can't tell you exactly,' offered Arno. 'But what we do know is that three days ago we were each minding our own business in Luxembourg . . .'

'Is that where you're from?' I asked.

'Indeed,' continued Arno. 'I run a market stall

in the city centre, and I bought a cup of rosehip tea from someone I didn't recognise.'

'And I own a guitar shop in the countryside,' added Wouter. 'And I also bought a cup of rosehip tea from someone I didn't recognise.'

'This person,' I said. 'Were they by any chance wearing a headscarf and sunglasses?'

Wouter nodded.

'Eva Klutsch,' I said.

'What?' frowned Wouter, sharing a look of disbelief with Arno. 'The president?'

'Has to be. Did anything about her strike you as unusual?'

Wouter thought for a moment, then said carefully, 'She did have a vibe.'

'What kind of vibe?' I pressed.

'A not-very-nice one,' replied Wouter.

'Anyway, that's the last thing we both remember,' said Arno, 'before waking up in Cloudberry Prison.'

'You were put to sleep,' said Tog.

'One hundred per cent,' added Fizz.

'I think you're right,' said Wouter, shaking his head in disappointment. 'The tea . . . it had a bitter taste to it.'

'Wait . . .' I said. 'Let me get this straight. It was the *real* Max and Ola I saw on the way to the party, and the *real* Max and Ola I saw outside our house. They must have been waiting for the chance to grab Dad! But you guys were the ones they found sleeping in a cave in the Arctic Hills! And because everyone thought Max and Ola were safely back in prison, the North Pole police stopped snooping around the village and they were able to put their evil plan into action.'

'We kind of got that ages ago . . .' said Tog awkwardly, not wanting to hurt my feelings.

'But I guess it doesn't hurt to recap,' said Fizz helpfully.

'Time's up,' said a prison guard, tapping his watch.

I thanked the two lookalikes, and we all stood to leave.

'May we ask our question now?' said Arno.

'Of course,' I replied. 'Fire away.'

'When can we go home?'

I suddenly realised how strange it must be for

Wouter and Arno to be snatched from the streets of Luxembourg and banged up in an elf prison at the North Pole. I wanted to say something encouraging, but I knew that the person who could definitely help them – my Dad – was in just as much trouble.

'I'll see what I can do,' I said, but my smile felt fake.

Anyway, I'm now at home, and I'm about to go to bed.

It's nearly twenty-four hours since my brothers and sisters left, but there's no sign of them.

Hopefully Dad has been rescued, and they are on their way home.

Monday 3 December

Steinar called in this morning with bad news. Last night, my oldest sibling, Whittle, tried to sneak into Castle Holstein, but got captured! The rest of my brothers and sisters haven't given up though, and they are going to try again tonight.

Steinar said we all have to carry on as normal, so I went to the Workshop to do my bit.

I could hardly concentrate, I'm so worried about Dad.

Tog saw how upset I was, and asked me how I was feeling.

Of course, I couldn't say anything, because the rescue mission is top secret.

Really glad I've got you, diary, to talk to, or I think I'd go a bit mad.

Tuesday 4 December

More bad news from Steinar. My second-oldest sibling, Sniff, has been captured too! I could see Mum was shocked, but she did her best not to show it.

'So what's the plan?' she asked.

'We carry on,' replied Steinar. 'Cog's the third oldest, and he's in charge now. He says he's going to need another twenty-four hours.'

'But what about the tour?' asked Mum. 'Torvil's due in Ottawa at a shopping centre in two days. Then a primary school just outside Milan. The children are going to be so disappointed. I suppose I could go, but I get so sleigh-sick.'

'We need you here, Mother Christmas, to help keep the elves calm and on track. There are still so many toys to make.'

I wasn't really part of the conversation, but knew I had to speak.

'What about Robot Father Christmas?' I asked. 'Maybe he could help?'

Steinar frowned.

'With respect,' said Steinar, 'that's the *very* last

resort. By the way, Holly.' He paused, choosing his words carefully. 'I'd like to try you in a different position within the organisation if I may? While we weather this storm.'

'What do you mean?' I asked.

'Your toy count,' said Steinar, reluctantly. 'It's dwindled almost to nothing. Every elf in the Workshop has to be on top form, or we'll never hit our deadlines.'

I looked at Mum, hoping she'd say otherwise. But she smiled sadly. 'It's probably for the best, Holly,' she said. 'We have to put Christmas first, remember?'

I nodded, knowing she was right.

'Don't worry,' said Steinar. 'There are plenty of other great jobs at Christmas Place. I'm sure we can find you something really fulfilling.'

Wednesday 5 December

I'm now a Clementine Elf, working in the Clementine Forest!

I've got one of the really important jobs, which is to carry buckets of reindeer poo from the slurry pit to the greenhouse, and pour it over the roots of the clementine trees.

Tog called by to give me some moral support.

I'm now a Clementine Elf, working in the Clementine Forest!

'Any tips?' I asked. 'I know you've got experience with reindeer poo, from when you worked in the stables.'

'Only one,' he said. 'You know that smell on your clothes?'

I sniffed my overalls. They were very pongy.

'What about it?' I asked.

'It doesn't come off,' he said.

Then after I went to bed that evening, something really important happened.

I woke up, because I heard voices. Steinar was at the door talking to Mum, and saw me sneaking down the stairs.

'Holly!' he said.

'What's going on?' I asked. 'Is there news about Dad?'

Steinar nodded gravely. 'Pickle and Sprocket,' he said.

I knew instantly what that meant. My fourth and fifth oldest siblings had been caught too!

'It's all under control,' added Mum. 'So don't worry. The rest of your brothers and sisters just need—'

'Another twenty-four hours?' I asked.

Steinar nodded.

'Mum,' I pleaded. 'Every time they try to get Dad back, one of them gets captured. And then they say they need another day. Soon there won't be any of them left. Please let me go and help them!'

'I can't, Holly,' said Mum.

'Why not?' I said. I wanted to cross my arms

and stamp my feet because I felt really angry, but somehow I managed not to.

'Because I need you to start practising,' said Steinar. 'With the sleigh.'

I frowned. 'What do you mean?' I asked.

'How else are you going to take that robot of yours on tour?' Steinar shrugged.

Now I can't sleep, so I'm under the covers with my torch writing this! I might not be part of the rescue mission, but at least now I get to help with my robot. And part of my job will be giving actual presents to actual children. I can't wait to see the looks on their faces when they receive their gifts!

Thursday 6 December

U p really early with Steinar, Fizz and Tog for sleigh training. Tog was beside himself with joy because Steinar asked him to steer!

It turns out he's been practising on the simulator all year, ever since he flew Dad's sleigh when we saved Christmas. It's a computer game Dad uses that makes it look like you're flying. Dad's been letting

Tog play on it for fun, but today he got to fly the sleigh for real!

When we were ready to leave for our first tour stop, Steinar sat up front next to Tog, and Fizz and I sat behind with the robot. Behind us were all the presents for the children we would meet on the tour.

'Check the sky is clear,' Steinar called to Tog. 'Then pull away when it's safe to do so.'

'Yah!' called Tog.

'Ho ho ho!' called the robot.

We all held on tight as the reindeer took off across the snow. All of us, that is, except the robot, who shot off the back of the sleigh, bounced off the sack of presents, and landed face down in a snowdrift.

We were halfway up in the air before we realised he wasn't there.

'Just like the real Father Christmas,' said Rudolph, as we prised the robot out of the snow. 'He always forgot to hold on, back in the early days. I once got to Cape Town before I realised he was flat on his bottom back in Christmas Place.'

There was a brief pause while I made the robot a seatbelt, then we gave it a second try. As soon as we were up in the air, Steinar gave Tog a Sleigh-Driving Exam, including an Emergency Stop in Mid-Air, and a Theory Test where he had to demonstrate his knowledge of International Aviation Protocols.

Luckily, he passed with room to spare, and the next thing I knew we'd dropped Steinar back at Christmas Place and we were taking off for Ottawa!

It was so exciting, riding the sleigh high over the Arctic mountains, across the Arctic tundra, down through Greenland, and across the cold, grey Atlantic Ocean to Canada.

As we came into land, we were joined by a flock of Canada Geese!

Soon we were circling a large city, and homing in on the long flat roof of an out-of-town shopping centre.

I could tell Tog was a bit nervous. But he did a brilliant job, landing with a bang on the snow-covered roof, and pulling the reindeer to a halt just before we reached the edge.

'Not bad,' called Rudolph over his shoulder, and Tog beamed with pride.

The manager was there to meet us, and led us down the back stairs to the ground floor of the shopping centre, where crowds of children were waiting.

When they saw the robot, dressed in his Father Christmas outfit and looking every bit the part, they cheered!

We set the robot up in the grotto, and Fizz brought the children in to meet him, one by one.

A small part of me felt a little bit mean for tricking them. But then, when I saw their smiles, I knew we were doing the right thing. After all, why should these children, who had been so good all year, miss out on meeting Father Christmas, just because Ola and Max had it in for my dad?

This afternoon's visit, in Milan, was a little more tricky.

The venue was a tiny bookshop in a back alley, with a sloping roof that was really hard to land on. And we also had a few problems with the robot.

He was meeting a nine-year-old boy called Fabio, who wanted to be an opera singer when he grew up, and sang the high bit from 'Nessun Dorma' to prove it. He was hoping for a dinner jacket as his main present so that he could wear it when he sang along to his favourite operas at home.

'I'll see what I can do,' said the robot, just like he was supposed to. 'Now let me give you a little something to be going on with.'

Only, when he handed Fabio the present, the robot wouldn't let go.

'Can I have it?' asked Fabio. 'Please?'

But the robot seemed to grip on even tighter.

'Don't forget to leave me a mince pie and a drink, and a carrot for the reindeer!' said the robot cheerfully, and his head started to spin round really fast.

Fabio's father tried to help, and with a superhuman show of strength, pulled the present out of the robot's hands. But the robot fell forwards and gripped his ankle instead, and Fabio's father was soon rolling around in agony, beating the floor in pain.

Luckily Fizz had the VR headset to hand, took control of the robot and powered him down. 'He needs resetting,' she whispered. 'Best to switch him on and off at least once a day. Or he gets a bit glitchy.'

'Is Father Christmas okay?' asked Fabio's father, staring back at the robot as I led it away from the grotto.

'He's a bit stressed,' I confided. 'With Christmas coming up.'

'That's some grip he's got,' said the father, hobbling slightly. 'I guess that's from climbing so many chimneys.'

Apart from that one little hiccup, though, everything went smoothly.

It was so amazing, seeing the happiness on all the children's faces. I'm such a lucky girl to be able to do this! Maybe next year Dad will bring me with him.

If we get him back, that is.

Friday 7 December

P hew! I'm exhausted.

I never realised Dad went to so many events in the run up to Christmas! The schedule Steinar's given us is packed really tight, and there's barely time for toilet breaks, let alone a chance to explore the countries we visit. He keeps calling Fizz on her mobile to check up on us, too, to make sure we don't miss anything – or anyone – out.

This morning we visited two more shopping centres. One in Dayton, Ohio, in the US and the other in Ghent in Belgium. On the outside, the children may have looked a little bit different, but on the inside they were exactly same, each and every one of them bursting with excitement to meet Father Christmas. Or rather, a robot that looked just like Father Christmas.

In the afternoon we visited a primary school in Nottingham in the UK, and after that we squeezed in a nursery in Kraków in Poland.

That's where I am now, in a hotel on the edge of the city, with the sleigh and reindeer parked on the roof.

No news of Dad. I'm worried that another of my brothers and sisters has been caught, and the rest have asked for another day to save him.

Saturday 8 December

Still no news of Dad.

Feeling quite tired so I'll just give you the headlines:

A shopping centre in Athens, Greece. An outdoor market in Paris, France. A creche in Niger City, Nigeria.

Sunday 9 December

No news.

The American School in Marrakesh, Morocco. A farmer's market in San Luis Obispo, in the US. A nursery in Madrid, Spain.

Dad's job is so hard!

Tuesday 11 December

Some kids somewhere. Then some other kids somewhere else. Still more kids, and more kids after that.

Wednesday 12 December

I AM SO TIRED.

Thursday 13 December

I HATE CHILDREN.

Friday 14 December

Woke up with a start. It's been a week now and no news of Dad, and we've been all over the world. Of course I've got the robot to remind me of him, but it's just not the same. In fact, the way he stands in the corner of my room at night, like a statue, never saying anything . . . It sort of makes me miss Dad more than if I was alone.

I met Fizz and Tog by the breakfast buffet, and together we went up to the roof of the hotel to find the sleigh.

When we got there, Steinar was waiting for us.

'How did you get here?' I asked.

'Public transport,' he said gravely. I could tell by the look on his face that whatever he had come to tell us, it wasn't good news.

'Who's been captured this time?' I asked.

'Thistle.'

Thistle is my sixth oldest sibling. Apparently he'd managed to get in and out of the castle several times without getting caught, but couldn't find Dad. The last time anyone had seen him, he was going to check the dungeons.

'So just Pocket, Snip, and Shard left?'

Steinar nodded. 'Obviously it's harder to do the rescue with just the three of them,' he said. 'So they've asked for ten more days. They're going to need to break into the castle a different way, which involves digging.'

'What?' I gasped. 'That'll take us right up to Christmas Eve! What if they *still* don't manage it? We have to get Dad back by then or Christmas will be cancelled!'

'I'm sorry, Holly,' said Steinar. 'We don't have a lot of choice.'

'But we do!' I protested. 'You could let me help with the rescue!'

'How?' asked Steinar. 'You can't even do this right.'

'What do you mean?' I asked. 'We're doing a great job!'

'There have been complaints,' said Steinar.

'What sort of complaints?'

'Fathers attacked. Presents held on to.'

'That was on the first day!' I protested. 'We had teething problems. But no one got hurt!' Then I remembered Fabio's father's bruised ankle. 'Apart from one person.'

'Which is why I'm here today,' said Steinar. 'To make sure it doesn't happen again.'

I was so flustered that I forgot to give the robot a reset before we set off. Which proved to be a big mistake.

Our first appearance of the day was at a retirement home in Reykjavík in Iceland. The grannies and grandads in the home had invited their grandchildren, and by the time we'd arrived, a large crowd had gathered in the TV lounge, all eager to meet Father Christmas.

The first few visits went fine. Then a little girl called Björk got up to meet the robot.

She was carrying a fizzy drink, and before we quite knew what was happening, the robot grabbed it and poured it all over his face!

Sparks began to fly out of his chest!

People started to scream as the robot ran around the retirement home, pushing over tables of cards, messing up jigsaw puzzles and chucking cosy-crime novels on the floor.

'Fizz, help!' I called. 'Shut it down!'

'I'm trying!' bawled Fizz. 'Nothing's working!'

Then the worst thing that could have possibly happened unfolded right before my eyes. Steinar tried to stop the robot!

'Hold it right there!' he bellowed, standing in the robot's way.

The robot toppled over, trapping Steinar underneath him.

'Help!' breathed Steinar. 'It's really heavy!'

Tog began to pull Steinar out from under the robot, not realising that the robot had grabbed hold of Steinar's trousers. Steinar slithered out, but his trousers stayed behind!

Luckily, Fizz finally managed to take control of the robot and powered it down.

'Cover me!' bellowed Steinar, and we all shielded him while he struggled back into his clothes.

Needless to say, he was not in a very good mood after that.

'I'll take charge from here, thank you very much,' he said, holding out his hands.

Fizz handed him the VR controls.

'Why?' I asked, looking at the robot. 'What are you going to do?'

'Bin it,' replied Steinar.

'But who's going to stand in for Dad?'

'I am,' said Steinar, fixing me with a stern look. 'I've got the wrinkles for it, apparently. We've got a primary school near Paris to attend in . . .' he glanced at his watch. 'Just under forty-five minutes.

So we need to get moving.'

'Wait!' I pleaded.

Steinar raised his eyebrows expectantly.

'It wasn't the robot's fault,' I insisted. 'I forgot to reset him. Tog, back me up.'

But Tog looked at me and shrugged. 'It would be pretty bad,' he said awkwardly, glancing at the robot, 'if it attacked a child. I mean, imagine.'

I couldn't believe Tog wasn't taking my side!

'I can fix him!' I exclaimed. 'I promise!'

'It's a nuisance,' broke in Steinar, 'and you're doing nothing of the sort. It's going in the bin, and you're coming with us to Paris.'

'No,' I said, shaking my head.

'No?' repeated Steinar.

'If he stays, I stay.'

Steinar gave a little laugh. 'Don't be ridiculous,' he said.

And then I ran away.

I was so upset I wasn't really looking where I was going. I couldn't believe that Tog hadn't stood up for me! Or that Steinar was going to throw away my beloved robot. I ran out of the retirement home, past some houses, and into a wood where I could be alone with my thoughts.

I heard Tog's voice calling me, and Steinar's, and Fizz's too.

But I was so cross I didn't answer.

After a little while I started to feel better, and went back. But the sleigh had gone! Instead, there was a note on official North Pole paper which read:

Dear Holly,

I am sorry that when I behaved perfectly reasonably, you overreacted and ran away. Please be advised that I have secured your room at the Meridian Inn Low-Cost Express for a week, and that we will collect you once we have completed the remaining dates of the tour.

Yours in elfship,

Steinar

Saturday 15 December

Can't believe I've messed up so badly.

Woke up late, and wandered around Reykjavík. All the Christmas lights are up in the old town, and you can see the excitement in everyone's faces, knowing that Christmas is coming.

Except I know it isn't.

Sunday 16 December

Don't feel like writing today, sorry.

Monday 17 December

r today.

Tuesday 18 December

Bleagh.

138

Wednesday 19 December

Found myself staring in the window of a little toy shop on the edge of town called Octavia's. There was a toy drone in the window, like the ones I made at the Workshop.

Or used to make.

Why did I ever think it was a good idea to make a Robot Father Christmas? I just don't have the skills.

Let's face it, I only got the job as a Christmas Elf because my dad's Father Christmas.

Thursday 20 December

Have decided that while I'm here, I might as well make myself useful. So this morning, I plucked up the courage to go into the toy shop I saw yesterday and ask for a job.

The lady who runs it is called Octavia and she sits behind a very high counter. So when I first said hello, she didn't see me.

'Down here,' I said. 'I don't suppose you're looking for an assistant?'

'Goodness!' exclaimed Octavia, peering over at me. 'Are you over seventeen?'

'Yes,' I said. 'By one hundred and thirty-eight and three-quarters.'

Octavia's eyes widened in surprise.

'I see,' she said uncertainly. 'Do you know anything about toys?'

'A lot,' I said. 'I used to be an elf in Father Christmas's Workshop.'

'How wonderful!' exclaimed Octavia. 'And you've bought a costume to match. That's just the kind of initiative we look for at Octavia's.'

Of course it wasn't a costume. I was wearing my

real clothes. But I decided not to tell Octavia that, as I've heard a lot of humans get freaked out by elves.

For the rest of the morning, Octavia trained me up as an assistant. She explained that before Christmas, lots of children visit toy shops, to try to decide what they'd like from Father Christmas. And that our job was to help them find the one special toy that would make the next year a truly exciting one.

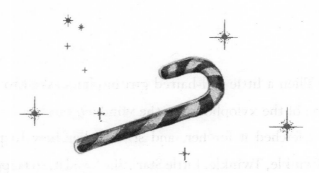

Friday 21 December

I can't wait to tell you what happened today!

It all started at Octavia's.

It was a really busy morning, with lots of children coming in with their parents and carers to look at toys. I'd been demonstrating all sorts of wonderful things: crafting sets, pirate ships, electronic diaries, in fact almost every toy you can think of.

Then a little red-haired girl in plaits asked to see one of the xylophones in the window.

I fetched it for her, and showed her how to play 'Twinkle, Twinkle, Little Star'. She loved it, so I tapped out 'Frère Jacques'. That went down well too, so I played 'Autumn Leaves' in the style of Oscar Peterson, the famous jazz musician. 'So?' I asked. 'Do you think you might ask for one from Father Christmas?'

She nodded. 'Can I tell you a secret?' she asked.

I leaned forwards so she could whisper in my ear.

'It'll be my first.'

'Christmas?' I asked in surprise. I was always very confused about how old humans were, and thought the little girl in front of me must be very young.

'No,' said the girl. 'I'm nine. So this Christmas is

my ninth. But this would be my first ever present.'

The surprise I felt must have shown on my face, because she didn't wait for my reply.

'I used to be on the Naughty List,' she said, lowering her eyes. 'But this year I've been good, for the first time ever.'

My heart skipped a beat.

'Wait . . .' I said. 'Is your name Taffeta?'

She frowned. Then she nodded. 'Taffeta Hound,' she said in a small voice.

I almost reeled over in shock. Could this quiet, gentle girl be the famous Naughty Lister who had once put her brother in the washing machine?

'I've got quite a temper,' she confessed, 'when I get going. But this year I've tried really, really hard.

'Wait . . .' I said. 'Is your name Taffeta?'

The xylophone's not for me — it's for my younger brother, to say sorry for being mean to him all these years. He's going to love it, I know he is.'

I felt a lump rise in my throat, like I wanted to cough or sneeze, or maybe even cry. But I didn't want to alarm Taffeta, so I hid my feelings as best I could.

'Don't worry, Taffeta,' I said. 'I'll let you into a secret. I'm a Christmas Elf, and I'm going to make sure Father Christmas brings you what you want.'

Taffeta beamed and handed me back the xylophone, then rejoined her family, giving her little brother a warm hug.

As soon as she had gone, I asked to see Octavia in the stock room.

'Thank you,' I said, 'for letting me see how children

make their lists. But I have an important job to do.'

'Don't tell me,' said Octavia wearily. 'You're going to work for some huge toy store. This always happens. One minute I train someone up, the next they're selling out.'

'No,' I said. 'It's nothing like that. I'm going to save Christmas.'

Octavia frowned and studied me closely.

'I don't think you are a Christmas Elf,' she said uncertainly. 'But if you were . . .' She looked around, as if to make sure no one was listening in. 'I'd want to say thank you. For helping all of these children's dreams come true.'

Moments later, I was out on the street, running through the falling snow to the last place I had seen

Robot Father Christmas: the retirement home. I had a hunch where Steinar might have left it, and sure enough, round the back by the kitchens, I saw a familiar-looking arm poking out of a wheelie bin.

Somehow, even though it was heavier than a sack of roasting potatoes, I managed to heave the robot out. I sat it up against a wall while I looked for its costume, which I eventually found in a black plastic bag covered with old cabbage. Last of all I found the VR headset and remote control that Fizz had made, tangled up in some old Christmas tree lights!

Soon I would have the help I needed to rescue Dad, and get Christmas back on track!

I brushed the robot's red velvet jacket down, powered it up, and the lights pinged on in its bright blue eyes.

'Ho ho ho,' the robot said. 'Hello.'

'Robot!' I exclaimed, throwing my arms around its neck. 'I missed you!'

'I missed you,' it repeated.

I couldn't believe my ears.

'You can speak!' I said.

'You can speak!' said the robot.

'Or can you?' I asked suspiciously. 'Maybe you're just repeating everything I say?'

'Goodbye,' said the robot. 'Don't forget to leave me a mince pie and a drink, and a carrot for the reindeer.'

I had a quick check of his circuits, but they were a complete mess!

Somehow, despite the melted wires and burnt plastic, he was still working. It was a miracle! The fizzy drink had somehow rewired him . . .

But there was no time to waste. We had to get to Holstein Castle before Christmas Eve, and without the sleigh, that meant travelling over land.

It also meant disguising the robot. Otherwise we'd be mobbed by children thinking he was Father Christmas!

As luck would have it, there was an old overcoat in one of the bins. It was a bit big, but once I brushed the potato peel off it and buttoned it up, the robot looked completely different. A little bit more crumpled, maybe, but a lot less like Father Christmas.

'Come on!' I said. 'We've got a boat to catch!'

'Come on!' repeated the robot. 'We've got a boat to catch!'

Saturday 22 December

Sorry if my writing is a bit shaky, but I'm writing this on the night ferry from Reykjavík to Amsterdam and the ship is bouncing on the waves.

To be allowed on, we needed to buy tickets. I knew the people in the ticket office would think I was too young to buy them, so I took the robot off to a quiet corner of the terminal to practise.

'One child and one adult, please,' I said in a loud, clear voice.

'One child and one adult, please,' repeated the robot.

'That's all you have to say,' I said.

'That's all you have to say,' said the robot.

Then we went up to the ticket window.

'Can I help you?' asked the assistant, brightly.

'What would you like for Christmas?' asked the robot.

'Excuse me?' said the assistant.

'I'll see what I can do,' said the robot.

The assistant frowned.

'Sorry,' I said, jumping in. 'My dad means, one adult and one child ticket, please.'

Reluctantly, she handed over the tickets.

'Ho ho ho!' said the robot.

'Are you harassing me?' asked the assistant, pointing to a sign next to the service window. It said: 'WARNING! We will not tolerate physical or verbal abuse towards our staff.'

I quickly led him away.

Sunday 23 December

On the train from Amsterdam to Luxembourg. Every town we pass through looks so Christmassy!

I was dealing out the cards for our first game of snap, when we were interrupted by the conductor.

'Tickets, please,' he barked.

'Are you harassing me?' asked the robot.

I was dealing out the cards for our first game of snap

'Ignore him.' I smiled as the conductor clipped our tickets.

'Goodbye!' said the robot, cheerfully. 'Don't forget to leave me a mince pie and a drink, and a carrot for the reindeer!'

'I think you've had quite enough already,' said the conductor.

I started dealing the cards.

'Ho ho ho!' said the robot, as if he was very happy with his hand.

I went first, and put down a two of clubs. The robot put down a five of diamonds.

'That's not how it works,' I said, handing him back the card. 'You either have to put down the next number, or the same suit. Or, if you can't put anything down, then you have to pick something up.'

'I'll see what I can do,' said the robot. Then he put down the three of hearts!

'Wow,' I said. 'You're good at this.'

'What would you like for Christmas?' he replied.

We were entering Luxembourg. Below us was a Christmas market!

'Look!' I said, nudging the robot. 'Isn't it beautiful?'

'Look!' he repeated. 'Isn't it beautiful?'

But although Luxembourg looked very Christmassy from the train, up close it was quite a different story. In the square outside the station was one of those giant Christmas trees they have in big cities, except all the needles had fallen off! The Christmas market was almost empty, and instead of looking bright and new, all the decorations were faded and old.

'Excuse me,' I asked a passer-by. It's hard to tell the age of humans, but I would guess he was around twelve years old. 'What's happened to the decorations?'

The boy looked around him, as if he was seeing them for the first time.

'Oh, those!' he said. 'You stop noticing them after a while. They've all been up since the summer.'

'So it's true?' I asked. 'About it being Christmas every day?'

The boy tipped his head from side to side and made a humming noise, as if he wasn't sure how to answer. 'Sort of,' he said. 'Only when it's Christmas every day, it stops being special.'

'Don't you get presents?' I asked.

The boy shook his head. 'We did to start with. Family presents. Not from Father Christmas. But it got boring, so we stopped.'

'Boring?' I asked. 'How could presents get boring?'

The boy shrugged and puffed his cheeks wearily. 'It just did,' he said. 'The more toys you have, the less you want to play with them. Same with Christmas cards,' he added. 'And decorations. Anyway, Happy Christmas,' he said half-heartedly. 'I've got to go and eat my two hundred and fifth Christmas dinner.'

'One more thing,' I said. 'Can you tell us where to find Eva Klutsch's castle?'

He pointed us in the direction of a coach stop.

When we arrived, we found that it was plastered with old posters, left over from the election. Each one showed an identical picture of Eva Klutsch, only this time without her headscarf and sunglasses. She had a strange look in her eyes, like she was angry and afraid. 'Vote Klutsch!' they said. 'And Have Christmas Every Day!'

'Hmmm,' I said thoughtfully.

'Hmmm,' repeated the robot, equally thoughtful.

'That,' I said, pointing at one of the posters, 'is the person behind all this. Dad's being held in her castle, and you and I are going to get him out.'

Monday 24 December

So much has happened today that I almost don't know where to begin.

We arrived in the mountains late last night. I was getting really stressed, because the journey took ages, and we were running out of time to save Dad. As the coach climbed higher and higher, twisting and turning on the narrow road, the clouds came in and it started to snow. We got out at the last village, called Bruchwalloon, which the driver told us was close to Eva Klutsch's castle.

The lights were off in all the houses, so the robot and I headed for the only hotel we could see, a place called Der Bierg Geess, which means 'The Mountain Goat' in Luxembourgish.

We pushed our way in through a revolving door into a large, dimly lit room with animal heads mounted on the walls. Faded paper chains criss-crossed the wooden ceiling, and a creepy old plastic Christmas tree stood by the reception desk, its baubles covered in dust.

It seemed like the place was empty, but when I went to ring the bell on the desk, a large red-faced man with an enormous grey moustache stood up from behind it, and introduced himself as Gustav, the manager of the hotel.

When I was signing for my room key, I happened to spot a Visitor's Book. Opening it, I saw all my brothers and sisters' names!

'Excuse me,' I asked. 'Are any of these people still here?'

Gustav shook his head. 'I'm afraid not. The last one to leave was . . .' he turned the book round on the counter top so that he could take a closer look. 'Shard Christmas,' he continued, 'Yesterday afternoon.'

Shard was the youngest of all my brothers and sisters!

I could guess what had happened.

One by one, all of my brothers and sisters had

tried to rescue Dad. And, one by one, they had all been caught!

'Your key,' said Gustav, handing me a large brass key on a tasseled fob. 'Will there be anything else?'

'Yes, please,' I said. 'Which way is Holstein Castle?'

'That way,' said Gustav, pointing with one of his sausage-like fingers. 'Further along the ridge. Come the morning, you'll be able to see it from your room.'

'We can't wait until then,' I said firmly. 'My whole family are in danger. I have to go now.'

Gustav sucked a lungful of air in through his teeth, then blew it out again through his moustache, its two ends floating upwards like the wings of a small grey bird. 'Impossible,' he said, 'the only way to get there is along the ridge, and the path is closed.'

'I can make my own path,' I replied.

'Not without risking an avalanche,' said Gustav, with a warning look in his eye. 'First thing in the morning, the Mountain Rangers will put charges of dynamite in the snow to make sure it's safe. Then they'll open the path. You've no choice but to wait.'

When we got to the room, I pulled back the curtains from the window. But there was just the dark window pane, and hurling snowflakes that pressed themselves to the glass like moths.

It was so frustrating! Dad was out there somewhere in the darkness, and so were my brothers and sisters!

The sound of running water pulled me out of my daydream. There was a bath tub in the middle of the room, and the robot was filling it! As I watched, a mound of soap suds spilled onto the wooden floor.

'What are you doing?' I asked.

'What are you doing?' repeated the robot, swinging one leg over into the water.

'STOP!' I yelled, yanking him out again. His foot was dripping wet, so I grabbed a towel, and dried it.

'What would you like for Christmas?' asked the robot.

'I'd like you to keep out of the bath,' I said. 'It's really bad for you.'

The robot glanced down at his foot, then nodded.

'I'll see what I can do,' he said.

There was no chance of rescuing Dad until the path to the castle was cleared, so I powered him down, plugged him in to charge, then tried to get some sleep. I couldn't help thinking about Tog and Fizz helping Steinar fill in for Father Christmas on tour. Even though they didn't know where I'd run off to, I wished that they'd tried a little bit harder to find me. I was all alone with only Robot Father Christmas to help.

Anxious as I was, I must have drifted off, because the next thing I knew, I was woken by the sound of far-off explosions. I raced to the window and threw back the curtain. The clouds had lifted and there, in the blue dawn, at the far end of a snow-covered mountain ridge, was Holstein Castle! It looked like something out of a fairy tale, with a jumble of grey-roofed towers and turrets, surrounded by a high wall.

There were more explosions, and an avalanche of snow went tumbling from the ridge, down into the next valley. Strung out along the ridge were half a dozen workers in bright-orange overalls, who I figured must be the Mountain Rangers that Gustav had told us about.

I threw on my clothes, chucked the VR headset in my rucksack and powered up the robot.

'Ho ho ho!' it said.

'Come on!' I squeaked, in a much higher voice than I intended. 'It's time to save Christmas!'

By the time we reached the mountain path, the sun was starting to rise, and the pale stone of Eva Klutsch's castle was burning gold.

'Look,' said the robot. 'Isn't it beautiful?'

I smiled in surprise. Was he taking in the scenery? Or just repeating something he had once heard me say?

'Yes,' I said, in case he had meant it. 'Very. But right now we need to focus on our plan.'

As I spoke, a light flashed on one of the turrets of the castle. I slipped on the VR headset, so that I could see through the robot's eyes, then zoomed in with the controls.

High on the battlements was a brightly coloured figure. He was holding a pike on a long stick, and the light was glinting off its metal blade.

I zoomed in closer.

It was a soldier. He had a strange, old-fashioned helmet, and was wearing a multi-coloured costume with a white ruff round his neck. I gasped. He must be one of Eva Klutsch's guards, from her private army!

There were flashes of light from the other turrets, and I saw that the whole castle was bristling with guards, each of them carrying the same sinister-looking pikes. No wonder all my brothers and sisters had been caught!

'What would you like for Christmas?' asked the robot.

'A way in,' I said, scouring the castle. The tallest tower was clear of guards. 'Come on!' I said, stowing the VR headset. 'We've got some hiking to do.'

Getting to the tower wasn't easy. We trampled along the snowy ridge to the castle, then edged along a narrow ledge at the bottom of the wall. As we turned the corner, we saw that there was a dark lake below us.

The robot and I tiptoed along in silence until we were directly underneath the tallest tower.

'Right,' I said, taking a deep breath. 'Here goes.'

I removed his coat, and straightened his red velvet jacket. Then I slipped on the VR headset, taking control of his body, and began to climb. All I could see was the brickwork in front of me – or rather, in

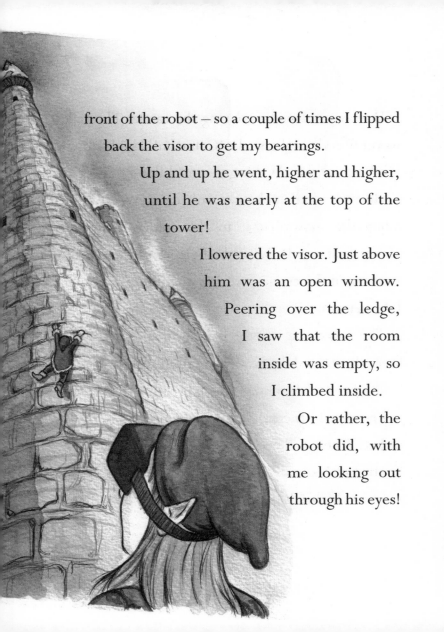

front of the robot — so a couple of times I flipped back the visor to get my bearings.

Up and up he went, higher and higher, until he was nearly at the top of the tower!

I lowered the visor. Just above him was an open window. Peering over the ledge, I saw that the room inside was empty, so I climbed inside.

Or rather, the robot did, with me looking out through his eyes!

I lost my balance, and tumbled forwards. I saw a flash of floorboard, then my display went blank.

I whipped off the headset and peered upwards. I could just about make out the open window. The robot must have fallen inside and damaged himself.

I began to panic. Was my Christmas magic running out?

I took some deep breaths.

'Believe in yourself,' I said firmly, remembering Dad's words. 'Holly Christmas, believe in yourself!'

Of course! I needed to restart the robot!

I powered him down with the controls, then up again. Nothing. Then a grey electronic flicker, and finally my vision came back.

As I watched through the headset, the robot ran

to the door and threw it open, then clattered down the spiral stone stairs all the way to the bottom of the tower, tiptoeing out into a large hall with what looked like a throne at one end, and brightly coloured tapestries on the walls.

I heard footsteps, and hid the robot behind a suit of armour as a troop of Holstein Guards rushed past.

Then, as they went, I spotted what I was looking for: an archway, with steps leading down!

As fast as the robot's metal legs would carry me, I raced across the hall, and headed down, down, down, until sure enough, I found myself in the castle dungeons.

There, on a small wooden table, next to a half-eaten pastrami sandwich, was a ring of keys. I heard a flush behind a nearby door. Whoever was guarding the keys must be in the toilet!

I took a deep breath and directed the robot to lift the keys up gently from the table so as not to make any noise, and tiptoed to the cells. It was almost pitch black, so I took a flaming torch from the wall to light our way. In the first cell, I saw my nine brothers and sisters sleeping soundly. In the second, also fast asleep, was my dad.

'Psst!' I hissed through the headset, as loud as I dared. Holding the torch high, I chose a likely-looking key and moved the robot to try it in the lock.

My father opened one eye, then closed it again. Then both his eyes sprang wide open.

'What the . . . ?' he asked, trying to figure out

why someone who looked just like him was trying to open the door to his cell.

'Dad, it's me,' I whispered. 'It's Holly! This is the robot,' I explained, 'that I made for the grotto. I'm controlling it from outside the castle.'

I tried the next key on the loop.

'Holly!' he said. 'Clever girl!'

'As soon as I find the right key, I'll get you out of here!'

'Halt!' called a gruff voice, and I turned the robot to see a bearded Holstein guard, his shiny pike lowered at me. 'Who goes there?'

I turned towards him, holding the torch high.

'Father Christmas?' He frowned. 'How did you get out?'

This was my chance! I worked the robot's controls, and pointed to Dad.

Then, as the bearded guard turned to look, I ran!

Up the stone steps I clattered, with the guard chasing behind me!

I reached the hallway, and sprinted towards the tower.

I bounded up more steps, taking two at a time. I was nearly halfway up, when I heard footsteps heading down towards the robot. Two more guards!

'Halt!' they called. 'Who goes there?'

I threw open a nearby door and raced along a gallery lined with family portraits, all of whom looked like Eva Klutsch.

Four more guards emerged from the door at

the far end of the gallery.

I looked back. The bearded guard was coming the other way.

I was trapped!

I turned round, looking for an escape.

Then I spotted it. Built into the panelling was a hidden door. I pushed through it, bolting it shut behind me, then scrambled up a spiral flight of wooden stairs to what appeared to be a trapdoor.

Grinning to myself, I made the robot throw back the trapdoor and we found ourselves on the roof.

Face to face with Max and Ola.

Ola frowned.

'Torvil?' he asked. 'What on earth are you doing here?'

I glanced around me. The entire Holstein Guard — the ones who hadn't been chasing me, that is — were gathered around us, each and every one of their pikes pointing straight at me.

'That's not him!' called the bearded prison guard breathlessly, emerging from the trapdoor behind me. 'The real Father Christmas is still in the dungeon.'

'Intriguing,' purred Max, stepping closer. 'Then what have we here?'

From inside the VR helmet, I saw his eyes search mine.

'Interesting,' said Max. 'This must be the robot our spy told us about.'

'Seize him!' ordered Ola, and my arms were gripped by two of the Holstein guards.

'What shall we do with him?' asked Max.

I heard a mechanical noise above us – a shiny black helicopter was coming in to land.

'We'll let Eva decide,' called Ola, looking upwards. Max called something in reply, but his voice was drowned out by the noise of the helicopter's engine. The wind from the blades was so strong that it blew one of the Holstein guard's ruffs off.

The blades stopped turning, the engine whined to a halt and Eva Klutsch removed her headset and stepped down from the cockpit.

'Welcome home, dearest.' Ola blushed, and the two of them shared an affectionate kiss.

'And how's my stepson-to-be?' asked Eva Klutsch.

Max also blushed, and gave an awkward little bow.

'All the better for seeing you, stepmother-to-be,' he smarmed.

Eva looked at Robot Father Christmas and frowned.

'And what's he doing here?' she asked. 'I thought we agreed. No exercise, no healthy food and no fresh air.'

'It's a robot,' said Max.

'We caught him trying to free Father Christmas,' said the bearded guard.

'A robot?' echoed Eva Klutsch, peering closer. Her eyes were cold and empty.

'They sent his sons and daughters,' said Max. 'And we caught them all. I think this –' he looked at Robot Father Christmas with disdain – 'is all they've got left.'

Eva Klutsch shook her head. 'Tragic,' she said.

'To think that pathetic family once had so much power. No matter. Tonight is Christmas Eve, and when the children of the world fail to receive their presents, their reign will be over!'

'Serves them right!' said Ola, clapping his hands and rubbing his palms together enthusiastically. 'This is where we finally get our own back.'

'I almost feel sorry for him,' said Eva. 'But then I remember how I waited – Christmas after Christmas, and no presents! How do you think that feels to a little girl, even if she is the naughtiest child in the world?'

'So what shall we do with the robot?' asked Max. 'Turn him into a novelty rubbish bin? Or a holder for walking sticks?'

'No,' said Eva, smiling. 'I have a better idea.'

She turned dramatically, her hands on her hips. 'What's the point in cannons if you can't fire them once in a while?'

For a moment, none of us understood. Then one by one, the penny dropped. Ola began to chuckle.

'Very clever, my darling,' he gushed. 'Very clever indeed.'

The next thing I knew, the guards were stuffing Robot Father Christmas into the barrel of a cannon!

'Light the fuse!' shouted Eva.

There was a hissing sound as the fuse burned down, then a loud bang, and everything went blank!

Down on the ground, I whipped off my VR

headset just in time to see the robot whistle over the battlements, rising high into the air, then arching down to land with a distant 'splosh' in the middle of the lake.

My heart began to race.

Water! That was the worst possible thing for an electronic robot!

I scrambled down to the water's edge, raced along the bank, and waded out into the shallows.

But I hadn't gone more than a few steps when a ripple appeared further along the shore, then a white bobble, then a red hat, then a familiar cheery face!

Soon the entire robot emerged, treading his way carefully up from the bottom of the lake.

Exhausted, he lay down on the pebble beach and I ran to his side.

'Are you okay?' I asked.

'Goodbye!' he said cheerfully. 'Don't forget to leave me a carrot. And a reindeer. And a mince pie for the drink.'

He closed his eyes.

'Don't go!' I begged, shaking him by the shoulders. 'Please, don't go.'

He opened his eyes again.

'Are you harassing me?' he asked.

'I need you,' I said.

'Your turn,' said the robot, gripping me firmly

by the arm and looking deep into my eyes. 'I've put down a two, so you put down a three.'

His head flopped back onto the gravel.

'Please,' I begged. 'I can't do this without you.'

The robot closed his eyes. 'You feel it, don't you?' he asked. 'That Christmas magic?'

There was a shower of sparks, and his body went limp.

He was gone!

I felt tears sting my eyes, and I hugged him tight.

'Goodbye, Robot Father Christmas,' I said. 'I'm going to miss you.'

For a few moments I sat there, staring out at the lake, listening to the waves lap the shore. What was I going to do now?

What was it the robot had said?

'*Your turn. I've put down a two, so you put down a three.*'

All right, the second part — the bit about the numbers — didn't make much sense. That was just something from our game. But maybe the first part, the bit about it being my turn, was him trying to tell me something.

He was right!

I couldn't sit there, moping. My whole family was in danger and, somehow, I had to rescue them, all on my own.

But how?

I glanced back at the castle, perched high above me. There was no way I could climb up the side of the tower like the robot. I didn't have that kind of strength. And besides, the battlements were crawling with the Holstein guards. That was why my brothers and sisters had all got caught.

There had to be another way in.

I stared out at the lake again, searching for inspiration.

Then it struck me.

The toilet flush! The bearded guard had been on the toilet next to the dungeons! Toilets meant pipes, and pipes meant sewers . . . and where better for sewers to empty than into a giant lake?

Without a second thought, I turned on my heels and sprinted towards the castle. But instead of climbing back up to the ridge, I scrambled across the rocks looking for . . . There! A tunnel!

I paused in the entrance, sniffing the air. It was really pongy.

But there was no time to waste. I pinched my nose tight and sloshed my way up a rocky passageway into the bowels of the castle, where a rusty iron ladder led up through a wooden manhole right into the corridor beside the cells.

'Holly!' gasped Dad, from behind the bars as I found his door.

'Shhh!' I hissed, putting my finger to my lips as I crept past him.

The bearded guard was back at his station, working on the second half of his pastrami sandwich, while the bunch of keys jangled on his belt.

As he opened his jaws to take a bite, I whizzed over with elf speed, unhooking the keys from his belt, and whizzing back again before he had time to blink.

'Holly!' gasped Whittle.

'Quick!' I said, unlocking his cell. 'I've found us a way out!'

'Hang on,' said Sniff. 'What's that smell?'

'Never mind about that,' I said. 'This is our chance to escape!'

'Did you get in through a sewer?' asked Cog, pulling a face.

'Where all the poo goes?' asked Pickle.

'Please, everyone!' I barked. 'Focus!'

'Yes, focus!' said Dad as I unlocked his cell too.

'For once in your lives, listen to your little sister!'

'Dear, oh dear, oh dear,' said a strange voice, and Max stepped out of the shadows. He was holding his nose to stop the poo smell, which made him sound funny. 'How you lot came to be in charge of Christmas, I'll never know.'

'Max!' I exclaimed. 'Back off! We're leaving, and you can't stop us!'

'Maybe I can't,' replied Max innocently. 'But my little sister can.'

'Little sister?' I echoed. Whatever did he mean?

As he spoke, someone stepped out from behind him, also pinching her nostrils and making a bit of a face.

It was Fizz!

My mouth fell open in shock. Now they were side by side, the resemblance was obvious. Even the way they held their noses was the same!

'But . . .' I stammered. 'But . . .'

'You thought we were friends?' asked Fizz, making a pretend sad face. 'No. And neither is this little guy. As she spoke, she flipped on a VR headset and began working the controls. Sure enough, a familiar red bobble hat emerged from the manhole, and the next thing I knew, the robot was staggering towards me like a zombie, his arms stretched out in front of him. He was alive after all! Although there was a strange look in his eye . . .

'But why?' I asked, backing away nervously.

'You took everything from us! Our factory, our

workers, even our home!' spat Fizz. 'Our father said.'

'He went bust!' exclaimed Dad indignantly. 'And ran off with the elves' pension fund!'

'But we thought you were our friend!' I protested, my back now against the door. 'You helped us make toys, and . . . Tog went to the party with you. How can you want to ruin Christmas for everyone?'

The next thing I knew, the robot had lifted me high up off the floor.

'Grab him!' yelled Dad.

'Do we have to?' asked Sprocket, screwing up his face in disgust. 'He's absolutely covered in poo!'

Dad jumped on the robot's back! But Fizz tweaked the controls, and the robot threw him against the dungeon wall.

'Stop!' I called. 'It's me, Holly!'

The robot paused, as if some part of him recognised me.

Fizz jabbed at the controls, but nothing happened.

'Ignore her,' I said. 'She can't control you. Not all of you, anyway. And especially not the part that loves Christmas.'

'What are you doing?' Max bawled at Fizz. 'Make him attack!'

'I'm trying to!' exclaimed Fizz. 'But nothing's working!'

'Give me those,' said Max, ripping the controls from Fizz's hands. It seemed to work, because the robot stretched out his hands again, and took a few hesitant steps towards me.

I took a deep breath, and focused on his twinkly blue eyes.

'Remember the Christmas lights we saw?' I asked.

The robot paused, and I could tell that he was listening.

'So beautiful,' said the robot. His head jerked from side to side, like it sometimes did when he got glitchy.

'These people,' I said carefully. 'The ones with the controls. They want to destroy Christmas.'

The robot turned to face Max and Fizz, who began to back away.

'We have to stop them,' I said.

'We have to stop them,' said the robot.

Max gave the controls one last stab, then threw them away.

'Run!' said Fizz. 'Before it's too late!'

Max and Fizz turned and ran, and the robot took off after them.

'Dad, Eva, run!' yelled Max, bursting into the Throne Room, where the two evil grown-ups were enjoying a glass of Luxembourg-made sparkling white wine. It took only one glance at the advancing robot, with the entire Christmas family in support, to send all four of the wrong-doers scrambling for the roof of the castle.

'Guards!' called Eva desperately. 'Guards!'

By the time we caught up with them, Max, Fizz, Ola and Eva were strapping themselves into the helicopter, surrounded by the entire Holstein Guard, pikes drawn.

The robot was doing his best to attack, but the

Holstein guards were ruthless, staving him back with their pikes.

'Next time, Father Christmas!' bellowed Eva as the rotor blades sliced the air. 'I'll have my revenge, you'll see!'

Then she worked the controls and the chopper lifted up into the air.

No sooner had it taken off, than Steinar and Tog arrived on the sleigh!

'Steinar!' bellowed Dad as soon as the reindeer had settled. 'What in galloping candy canes are you doing here?'

'I've come to pay the ransom,' explained Steinar. 'I've got all the presents, look.'

'We thought it was the only way to get you back,'

called Tog, looking worried.

'No need.' Dad beamed. 'Thanks to Holly, once again, Christmas has been saved!'

And that was that. Dad snatched up the reins, shouted instructions to the reindeer, and took off into the darkening sky.

There was a pause, while we all watched him go, off to deliver presents to children all around the world.

'Holly, I am so sorry,' said Steinar. 'I owe you an apology.'

'So do I,' said Tog, looking down at his feet. 'I looked everywhere for you after you ran away, but then we had to carry on with the tour. You wouldn't have wanted us to stop meeting the children.'

'We're sorry, too,' said Whittle, gesturing to my eight other brothers and sisters.

'That's okay,' I said.

'Can I say something else?' asked Tog, looking at Whittle.

'Please,' said Whittle.

'Holly's magic is really special. And you guys have to stop leaving her out of things just because she's the youngest.'

There was a pause, where it seemed as if no one knew quite what to say.

'Does anyone have a reply to that?' pressed Tog.

The robot blinked twice, then spun its head all the way round. 'What would you like for Christmas?' he asked.

Everyone laughed.

Then there was another pause, as we all realised we were stuck in Luxembourg with no way home!

Tuesday 25 December

It's Christmas!

It was so lovely to wake up in my own bed and to see my stocking at the bottom of it, stuffed with presents!

To think that everywhere in the world, children were doing the same thing: tearing open their presents and fizzing with wonder at the magic of Christmas.

But I need to fill you in on how I got home.

Luckily, just after Dad took off in the sleigh to deliver the presents, a police helicopter landed. Apparently one of the neighbours had complained about the noise, and the entire Holstein Guard were taken in for questioning in connection with the firing of an antique cannon.

Once they'd all been processed and ferried away in a succession of armoured cars, the police gave us a lift to Luxembourg airport, where we jumped on a flight to Svalbard in Norway, up in the Arctic Circle.

Steinar had called ahead, and as soon as we were through the baggage hall, a flotilla of elf-driven dog sleds whisked us across the ice to the Arctic Hills, where Mum was waiting for us at Christmas Lodge.

Mum was waiting for us at Christmas Lodge

By then it was way past my bedtime, so I hung up my Christmas stocking and went straight to bed.

Now it's time to go downstairs and see what I got for my main present!

You'll never guess what I got.

A basketball hoop!

It was exactly what I wanted. Dad fixed it to the wall outside and I've been shooting baskets all morning. Arno and Wouter, the two lookalikes are here too. After Steinar got them out of prison this morning, he invited them for Christmas lunch. They are really friendly, but have both sworn never to

touch another drop of rosehip tea, no matter how aromatic it is.

And that's not all. There was a surprise gift too!

Of course, I could guess from the wrapping – there aren't many presents that are exactly the same size and shape as your own father – but when I opened it, and knew for sure, I jumped for joy!

It was Robot Father Christmas! But he was all shiny and new. Apparently Steinar spent all night in the Workshop giving him a complete makeover. They must have given his insides a tune-up too, because the light had come back in his eyes. Literally.

'Robot!' I cried. 'We're never going to be apart, ever ever again! I think I'm going to call you Robie.'

'Are you harassing me?' he asked.

Anyway, I've got to go because Tog's arrived, and we're going to teach Robie to ice-skate.

BEN MILLER is the author of magical stories including
The Night I Met Father Christmas
The Boy Who Made the World Disappear
The Day I Fell Into a Fairytale
How I Became a Dog Called Midnight
The Night We Got Stuck in a Story
Diary of a Christmas Elf
Secrets of a Christmas Elf

He is an actor, director and star of the hit comedy the Armstrong and Miller sketch show, as well as appearing in the Paddington films, BBC's Death in Paradise and the Netflix smash, Bridgerton.

@actualbenmiller

BEN MILLER is the bestselling author
of magical stories for all the family:
The Night I Met Father Christmas,
The Boy Who Made the World Disappear,
The Day I Fell Into a Fairytale,
How I Became a Dog Called Midnight,
The Night We Got Stuck in a Story,
Diary of a Christmas Elf and
Secrets of a Christmas Elf.

He is an actor, director and comedian, best-known for the
Armstrong and Miller sketch show, the Johnny English and
Paddington films, BBC's Death in Paradise and
Netflix smash, Bridgerton.

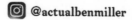 @actualbenmiller

ENTER A
WORLD OF WONDER
WITH CLASSIC ADVENTURE FROM BESTSELLING
BEN MILLER

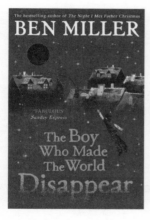

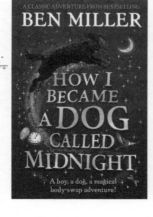

FESTIVE BESTSELLERS FROM
BEN MILLER

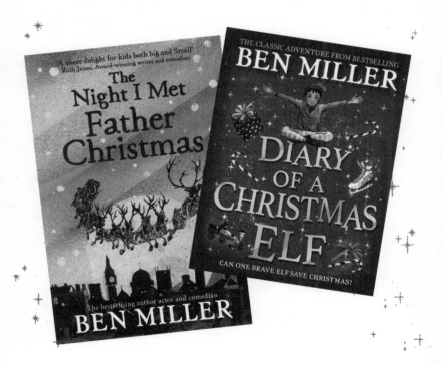